MILROY GOES

Passear

Seven Chapters, Unforgettable Moments, Wisdom to Hold Close.

Passear *written by* Milroy Goes

First printing. 2025

ISBN: 978-81-948285-0-1

First Edition: 7th April 2025

Cover Design by Milroy Goes, in Lisboa, Portugal.

Publication: Buenos Muzik

www.milroy.goes.co.in

Merchandise: linktr.ee/PASSEAR

Disclaimer

This book is a work of observation, speculation, and occasional exaggeration. While inspired by real-life encounters, all characters, events, and conversations have been filtered through the author's wildly overactive imagination. Any resemblance to actual persons, living or persistently messaging, is purely coincidental—or possibly just unfortunate.

No feelings were harmed in the making of this book (as far as I'm aware), but should you find yourself identifying with any character, take it as a sign that you, too, have led an interesting life.

Read responsibly, laugh freely, and if anything sounds suspiciously familiar… well, let's just say it's probably not about you. Probably.

The book is dedicated to my parents,
Mãe - Piedade Cardoso
and *Pai* - Vicente Floriano Gois

...who raised me to be a man capable of dealing with any situation in life.

I.

Foreword

Travel for me has always been an adventure, an expedition into the unknown, exploring new places, their history, architecture, landscapes, and most importantly – people. But when travel gets peppered with a spot of romance, the experience becomes surreal – the stuff of movies and books.

In the pages of 'Passear', budding filmmaker Milroy Goes takes you into a journey of soul-searching and passion. A happy-go-lucky bachelor's drifting sojourn into self-discovery while discovering the world.

I was absorbed, sucked into the very real yet dream-like world of these pages, created from the author's real-life experiences, the book took me to the sun-kissed beaches of Goa and across the Atlantic to London, Lisbon, Los Angeles and beyond. Once I finished the book, I was left with a bittersweet feeling, I wish the book hadn't ended, and the journey could go on...

Manish Gupta

Film Director / Writer / Producer

ⓘ

Manish Gupta is an Indian film director and screenwriter known for his work in the Bollywood Film industry. He began his career by writing the screenplay and dialogues for the 2005 film *Sarkar*, starring Amitabh Bachchan. Gupta made his directorial debut with a segment in *Darna Zaroori Hai* (2006) and went on to direct films such as *The Stoneman Murders* (2009), *Hostel* (2011), *Rahasya* (2015), *420 IPC* (2021), and *One Friday Night* (2023). His writing credits also include the legal drama *Section 375* (2019). Gupta is recognized for crafting suspense dramas inspired by real-life events.

III

II.

Foreword

For us in Goa when we were growing up, "Passeio" meant a bike ride in the evening with my three best friends, one of whom became a renowned High Court Judge, and another became an engineer and a ship-builder and the third one became a teacher. But in our youth in early seventies, we would go pedalling on our bikes and go on our daily ride from Cuncolim to Assolna bridge and then come back from Chinchinim via Panzorkonn and Kanknnam Moddi and that ride was replete with conversations about local Goa politics, world news and other interesting current fare.

But with today's generation it's entirely a different story. Goans don't ride bikes any more. They are no longer in Goa but wander all over the world. And that's where the idea of this book "Passear" came into being. Our talented creative artist/director/thinker went around the world crossing the seven seas and made a collection of his sojourns and brought them out in book form in this beautiful creative oeuvre and aptly named it "Passear".

I have not read the book yet, but I can surmise its interesting contents, which will be very elucidating for the readers.

Milroy has created artistic paintings, has done critical film work and directed films in his passionate creative field and has now embarked on creative writing.

I can anticipate a great demand for his work and I am sure the readers will get their utmost satisfaction to their heart's content.

I wish all the success and fame to Milroy Goes in this endeavour.

Silviano Barbosa

Author of the Canadian/Goan Novel, "The Sixth Night"

Preface

One evening during my church small group Christmas dinner in 2024, at the dinner table with my church group in Los Angeles—eight of us in total—we gathered for a meal organised by the group. As we waited for our dinner and enjoyed the starters, we found ourselves engaged in lively conversation, sharing our backstories, love stories, and amusing encounters in the world of dating. I recall sharing a few short yet intriguing stories, many of which you will find in this book. My friends found them fascinating, and though I had many more to tell, time was short. I decided to save some for another day.

I'm a very shy person, but if I decide to talk, I open up and instantly make interesting conversation and friends. If I decide to pull the blanket of shyness over myself, I ignore everyone in the room. Many people say I have met very interesting people—celebrities, billionaires—and I believe it is to do with my shyness. Indeed, it is. And secondly, my fame.

Then, during a business trip and holiday in Lisbon, Portugal, after an unexpected encounter with a complete stranger, the idea of writing a book about these experiences began to take shape. The book was later edited and revised while I was holidaying in Tenerife, in the Canary Islands, Spain. The cover design was created upon my return to Lisbon from Tenerife.

As a filmmaker and writer, my profession as a Film Director has taught me to study human behaviour—a subject I find particularly close to my heart. Understanding people, their habits, and their patterns is something I have always been keen on. I remember watching the Hollywood film *Fame*, where an instructor advised students that to master method acting, they must observe people. That scene left a lasting impression on me in the early days of my career, and I have since incorporated that practice into my own work—whether writing film scripts, developing characters, directing films, or guiding actors through method acting. Through years of keen observation, I have developed a deep awareness of the people I meet and their subtle behaviours.

This book is not intended as a scientific study of human behaviour, nor should it be considered formal research. Rather, it is a collection of my personal experiences and reflections on the people I have encountered.

Perhaps, within these pages, you may find situations that resonate with your own experiences—unanswered questions that finally make sense. If nothing else, I hope this book serves as an enjoyable read and offers a glimpse into the intricate world of human interactions.

Table of Contents

1.

Beyond the Profile: Meeting Strangers in a Digital World

A Galão, Pastéis de Nata, A Stranger, and A Mystery

When meeting a stranger turns into an unexpected observation of human behaviour.

After a decade of not using a famous app to meet travellers around, I found myself in Lisbon and decided to reactivate my account—just to see if I could meet a fellow traveller. I browsed through those travelling to Lisbon. Most had unverified accounts, so I decided to send one common message to the girls I found prettier—naughty of me. The message was simple:

"Hello, would you fancy Galão coffee and Pastéis de Nata?"

Ten hours later, I received a reply from a Croatian girl: *"Where?"* I told her I was near Praça do Comércio. She asked, *"Which city?"*

"Lisbon."

She said she'd be in Lisbon the next day. True to her word, the following morning, she messaged me her phone number on the app. About ten minutes later, I sent her a Text message. She started chatting right away, asking where I was and what my plan was.

Lisbon wasn't new to me—I'd been here several times and knew the area well. My younger brother Rohan was with me, like a bodyguard, knowing the ins and outs of the city. The Croatian girl sent me her location pin; she was right in Praça do Comércio, about a 30-minute walk away. She said she was there and wanted to explore the city. That plan certainly didn't include me, as she made her own intentions clear while asking about mine. I was only in it for coffee, curious to see what meeting a complete stranger would be like over this app. She said we could meet anytime, so I sent her my location so she could gauge the distance and plan accordingly.

She was having breakfast when she messaged, which gave me the perfect opportunity to get ready, as I had only just woken up. It was late in the morning—we had been changing our Stays while waiting for business confirmations in Lisbon and looking to book tickets to London. Since that wasn't happening soon, my brother and I spent our days walking around Lisbon, hopping into different coffee shops, and indulging in Pastéis de Nata. And so the previous night we slept quite late exploring the Lisboa.

I decided to keep her occupied instead of making her wait for me. *"Oh well, enjoy your breakfast. Lisbon is an amazing place. I'll leave in 20 minutes."*

That evening, I had also committed to a church dinner. My brother and I had found a wonderful Christian church in Lisbon, and we never missed a Sunday service. They had planned a dinner on Wednesday, so I signed up. I told the Croatian girl about it so she would know I was only available during the day.

The previous day, while in Alfama, we had discovered a lovely café "Basbousa Café" run by a kind-hearted Tunisian woman. Her hospitality lingered in my mind. So, when the Croatian girl asked where I wanted to meet, I immediately thought of Alfama and that café. I sent her the Geo location, letting her navigate her way there. For those unfamiliar with Alfama, it's a picturesque, uphill, and one of the most traditional neighbourhoods in Lisbon. It's beautiful, but quite a workout with its steep ascents and descents—you hardly realise you've walked 2–3 kilometres. I often go there for a galão at one of the charming local cafés, and occasionally in the evening to enjoy some lovely fado. I once had the pleasure of witnessing Goan *fadista* Sonia Shirsat perform at a fado restaurant.

She was playful over text. When I sent my location, she responded, *"It will take me 20–30 minutes. You will need to wait for me then, hahaha."* Then another: *"I'm walking slowly because I am dead, hahaha."* I found her humour amusing.

After some waiting and sipping coffee at the café, I received a message from her: *"I'm walking. I have 20 minutes to this coffee."* I replied, *"Not a problem, I'm here. I think I walk really fast."* In reality, I was used to the incline because I live in Los Angeles, on a hill. A similar incline is quite common when I go hiking, except that Lisbon has steps.

Her response felt rude: *"No, you just chose it. Very long way for a coffee shop."*

Well, she *had* asked me to choose, hadn't she? As a gentleman, I did.

Then came the rudest part—a voice note: *"Look, I am walking, and I still have another 20 minutes because I need to go up and down stairs. Honestly, no point in coming there because*

I've already been walking for more than 30 minutes, and I'm dead." She exhaled dramatically. *"So, I will cancel this."*

Her tone set off a red flag. But this wasn't a date, so I ignored it. I still wanted to meet her, if only to prove my instincts right. My brother, unaware she was a complete stranger, asked if my friend was still coming. I hadn't told him the truth—I said she was a friend, otherwise, he wouldn't have let me go meet her. He wanted to spend time with me, as we were meeting after a year. But he waited.

After hearing her voice note, I hesitated. Should I tell him she cancelled? I don't easily give up once I commit to something. If I can fix a situation, I will.

So, I messaged her: *"Okay, I'll find a spot near you. No worries, I totally understand."* Then, as a gentleman, I apologised: *"Sorry if I upset you. If you still have time, I'll walk towards you. Perhaps today is my last day in Portugal. I'm travelling back to London, then to Los Angeles. Cheers!"*

Why did I feel the need to share my travel plans? I don't know.

I wasn't sure how keen she was, but I was quite optimistic that she would consider my apology. Why did I even need to apologise in the first place? Well, as a gentleman would, I did so to ease the situation. Secondly, I knew my brother would find it absurd that a friend had messaged to meet up and then simply ghosted. I was caught in a situation where I had to please both sides. Moreover, I was very inclined to make it clear that I wasn't insisting on a meeting point that was only convenient for me.

A minute later, she sent me her location pin—another café, just 10 minutes from where I was. She was very close by, and it wouldn't have made sense for her to give up over such a short distance. Well, I informed the Tunisian lady, the owner of the café, that my friend wasn't up for the climb, so I was heading down.

When I arrived, it felt like a scene from a mystery spy film—an underground café. Yes, the place was almost like a basement, but with beautifully artistic old walls. The only girl immediately visible as I walked down the steps into the café was her—a pretty blonde in a white, elegant coat. I recognised her from the photos on her travel profile. I wasn't entirely sure if she was the one, but I was prepared to approach her. And if she wasn't, well, I might have ended up meeting a complete stranger instead.

Well, as I approached, I noticed a man in black hoodie type pullover, and in black jeans nearby, making me wonder if he was watching me. But that was a thought for later.

I walked up to her like a gentleman with absolutely nothing to lose—something like James Bond would—and said, "You must be Ana." She looked surprised at my confidence.

Seated, she extended her hand for a handshake without standing. There was only one chair at the table, almost like a perfect setup, even though the table was meant for four, just like the others. The two extra chairs had simply been placed on the other side, possibly on purpose.

So my brother pulled another one. Her English accent was similar to Russian or Ukrainian—unexpected from a Croatian as I thought.

I asked if she had ordered any beverage or snacks. She sighed, *"I've been sitting here quite a long time, and no one came to take my order."* I tell you, it's a blatant lie, but men often play along. That's where the Gentleman code gets activated; the Code: "If she lies, don't expose her. Simply play along, letting her believe she has deceived you—after all, that's what she expects."

I asked what she would fancy. She requested a cappuccino, so I went straight to the counter. It's a posh cafe, have really good coffee, snacks, and staff. The server suggested that I sit and she would come to take the order, but I preferred ordering directly. My brother and I got another round of Galão.

When the coffee arrived, she asked the waitress about the toilet and left to the toilet. What I carefully noticed was that she had left her coffee unattended. Her belongings were on the seat, I felt it was a strange move when meeting a stranger. A man in the corner kept watching. She returned with two sugar sachets and a stirrer. Had she really gone to the loo, or just to get sugar?

We had a conversation over coffee, but she was mysterious —revealing little about herself. At some point, I noticed the man in black still lingering nearby. I have never met any stranger who have been so secretive, so I was very curious.

And the very purpose of this was to become friends, not to remain complete strangers.

We were talking about ourselves, and I thought I should start a topic to introduce myself. She claimed to work in PR and marketing, she stated that she owned her own business in marketing and did not work for any company. She also claimed she marketed notable brand that you see on all across the media, she claim once she had a chance to market that brands product on her own. It's a significant accomplishment for anyone to claim. When I asked if I could see her work, she made a dismissive gesture and said, "I have nothing to show. It's everywhere." That was clearly just a lipstick stain on a coffee mug[1].

It reminded me of someone I had met on a flight—a British girl studying in Canada—while I was travelling from Los Angeles to London. She was my co-passenger and had mentioned owning her own company. However, unlike Ana, she had a business card and several publications on social media that I could see. I brought up this story to Ana so she would know that I had met someone similar, but with actual proof of her work.

Whenever I introduce myself, I am often asked if they can see my work, and it is always available on some streaming network that I can point to. But this Croatian girl was just creating something, perhaps to fit her narrative.

Before that, I told her about the company my brother and I own, showing her a bit of our social media work—what we were doing at the time to promote musicians, singers, and authors.

After finishing our coffee, she said she wouldn't eat until sunset. A cue for me to wrap things up. I paid the bill, and she thanked me. When I stood to say goodbye, she remained seated, extended her hand, and shook mine gently. This is one of those meetings where I don't feel quite sure about taking a selfie, and yet, I just couldn't be bothered to take one.

As we walked away, my brother and I analysed the encounter, and a thought arose that we decided to discuss later:

Who was the man lurking nearby? He was surely with her. She might have been one of those girls who pretend to be alone. While this wasn't a date, she could have easily introduced her companion. I've met travelling couples before—I've even hosted some in the past.

Was she just looking for free coffee? Was she really interested in making friends? Why didn't she turn up at the location I sent and instead asked me to meet her at the location she preferred? Why did she stand up and leave her coffee unattended? She surely knew she had someone to watch over her belongings and coffee.

That night, we didn't make it to the church dinner party, as we were quite far from the meeting point—or it would have been another chapter of meeting strangers.

I would normally write a review about the person I met on their profile, but I chose to instead write a text message.

Later that night, I sent her a message:

"Boa noite, Ana. I've met a few people through the travel app, and they've all been genuinely respectful. I'm thankful for your time and the conversation. Bon voyage! Have a wonderful year ahead. If our paths cross, we shall raise a toast over another coffee. Until then, Adeus!"

Translation: You were creepy, not very respectful, and I hope we never meet again.

One thing I've learned while travelling: People who travel a lot tend to be either very rude or very polite.

2.

A Valentine's Day Twist: An Unexpected Encounter

A Solo Journey, Colva Beach and a New Friendship.

A chance encounter, a solo journey, and a Valentine's Day that turned into an unexpected adventure.

It was in the early days of using Social Media Network to meet random people – possibly a fluke. That doesn't happen much after the Dating Apps era, but I bet I don't do Dating Apps. It's not my space for now.

So, I met a girl locally, within Goa, about 20 kilometres away from my town. We met a couple of times over coffee and beach walks, and had developed a good friendship, which could potentially lead to something more.

On Valentine's Day, I thought I'd ask her out. I didn't have my own scooter or car, and of course, I wasn't driving a car, so I borrowed a scooter from my neighbour. I had the scooter for the whole day, and I would return it the next day. With that plan in mind, I had sketched out a really nice 14th of February.

I messaged her, and she agreed to be my Valentine. We set a meeting point at a café in Margão, opposite the Margão Kadamba Bus Stand. This was the era when I used an Old Keypad phone, with no internet, and every text message would cost me. Calling and messaging weren't as privileged as they are now, but still, we were progressing into the digital world. Maybe I didn't have a better phone then, so it wasn't completely black and white.

I waited for her at the café for a very long time. My calls weren't answered, nor were my messages replied. I sat alone at my table, sipping coffee, while I noticed two girls on the other side of the café table. They seemed to either know me or were talking about something else, but I found it interesting that they kept looking towards me and laughing. I thought I would just go up to them to talk.

Then, just as I was about to get up, the girl I had been waiting for messaged me, saying she wasn't feeling well. I vaguely remember her saying her mum wasn't well. Whatever the reason, she had clearly called off the date. I felt disappointed as I had planned the whole day.

At the time, I ran my own business, developing websites and promoting businesses on Search Engine Optimisation listings. I was completely independent. I'm still that way, but back then I was more of a businessman and less of a filmmaker. I had made a few short films and my successful debut feature film by that point — we're talking about 2012. I had my own money, my own time, and nothing to lose. All

I wanted was good company to spend the rest of the day with, especially since I had borrowed the scooter-bike, which would have been a complete waste if I returned it to my neighbour that same evening.

Just then, I noticed a Japanese girl in a beautiful red dress, with a large backpack. As she pulled the café glass door open, her long dress flowed beautifully in the breeze. She sat right next to my table, alone, pulled out a travel book, ordered a coffee, and jumped straight into the chapter on "Goa", possibly to read about the place she was in.

That was my cue. I thought I'd have a fine reason to approach her. As soon as we exchanged glances, I said, "Would you mind if I join you?" (Translation: I want to sit next to you.)

She said, “Sure,” and I took my cup of coffee, glancing at the girls seated in the corner of the café. I thought to myself, well, she's definitely prettier than those girls in the corner. I'd never met a Japanese girl before, so I figured I'd rather sit next to her.

Once I sat down, I asked, "What are you looking for in the book?" She explained that she had just arrived in Goa by bus and was searching for what to do while she was here. Unfortunately, she only had an 8-hour layover before her next bus, which would take her to the next state in India. She wasn't planning to stop in Goa and was regretting not making more plans.

As she flipped through the pages, I noticed "Colva", which was very close to where we were. I pointed to it and said, "Would you fancy going there? I can take you; I have a bike."

She hesitated, saying, "I'd love to, but I have a huge backpack. How would you keep it on the bike?" I quickly replied, "We can leave it here at the café."

She seemed surprised, "How can that be safe?" she asked. She was so kind and cautious. I reassured her, saying, "Goa is a safe place, at least to me." I then asked the café waiter, and he agreed to look after her bag, storing it behind the cash counter. She grabbed her purse, and we took off.

While riding to Colva Beach, she remarked, "You're a safe rider," noticing that I was being particularly cautious with my scooter riding skills. I was, of course, extra careful, especially since I didn't have a driving license. I wanted to make sure there were no patrolling police or unexpected situations that could land me in trouble. But she didn't know that; we were riding nice and easy, following all the rules. I wore a helmet, and so did she – I had come prepared for the evening.

As we reached the parking area, I took off my helmet and said, "Check this – when we come back from lunch, this helmet will still be here, and I bet no one will steal it." She believed me, and so did I. I knew one thing for sure: Goa, though small and diverse, is a safe place, especially among the migrants and different ethnic groups who know that Goans trust easily.

I took her to a lovely beach shack called "Luke", where we had a delicious lunch. As we began talking about our lives, she mentioned that she was married, and as a gentleman, I immediately kept my distance, following the unwritten Gentlemen code of never intruding into someone else's relationship. "Treat others as you would want your own loved ones to be treated," I thought.

The conversation continued, and what truly struck me was her humble behaviour and complete trust in a stranger. When she asked what I did, I casually said, "Why don't you search my name on internet and see?" I told her my name, and she was amused to find me on search engine. She pulled out her phone and searched me, and it wasn't long before she exclaimed, "Wow, you're a famous personality!"

She wasn't any less remarkable herself. She was an TV host in Japan, and I was amazed by her distinct achievements. We exchanged our Social Media network details before I paid the bill. She was genuinely grateful for the lunch, and we took a long walk along the beach. As we strolled along the shore, chatting and enjoying the scenery, I kept an eye on the time, knowing I needed to drop her off before her bus departs.

She mentioned that her husband loved collecting swords, or perhaps I imagined that part. I wasn't quite sure, but it seemed her husband was a nice man, and she was a solo traveller, exploring India from south to north. She had never planned on stopping in Goa, yet there she was, experiencing it for a few hours. She did mention that if I ever visited Japan, I must come and visit them. Japan is definitely on my travel list!

An hour before her bus was due to depart, I reminded her that we should leave. We walked back to the scooter and, sure enough, the helmets were still there, untouched. She was surprised and said, "Goa really is a safe place." When we returned to the café, her bag was safe and intact, just as we had left it. She was visibly happy and relieved.

It was then time to say goodbye. As we walked out of the café, there were many men around the area, usually taxi drivers or bike pilots[2]—a common sight in that part of town. As they saw her, I noticed tears roll down her cheeks. She had genuinely enjoyed the time spent together, and honestly, so had I. The men around us, however, assumed we were a romantic couple bidding farewell, and one of them, sensing the moment, said, "Just kiss her."

He thought we were lovers bidding goodbye on Valentine's Day. Little did they know, I had been stood up, and I had asked this random girl out. On her part, she had been waiting at the café for 8 hours until her next bus, but in those hours, she got to explore a little part of Goa.

She was a great solo traveller, very polite, and we are still connected on Social Media network. The last time she messaged me, she called me "brother".

3.

A Flight to Remember Day

Old Money Style, Cheese and a Business Card.

A Chance Encounter at 30,000 Feet.

It was a cool winter in Los Angeles in early 2025, and I had plans to visit my sister in London. Part of my visit was for business, and partly to see my sister Sera, my brother-in-law Manuel, my niece Hannah, my nephew Hezron, my mentors Anthony Coombs-Humphreys and Christine, as well as my producer Manna Mohie. I had been looking forward to seeing them for quite some time.

I booked my flight and found one that went from Los Angeles to Canada, and then from Canada to London. I hadn't realised that I would need to apply for an ESTA visa for transit before the flight, but luckily, as my instincts suggested, I signed up for the ESTA visa just in time.

When I arrived in Canada, I had quite a long wait before boarding my flight to London. As boarding time approached, I joined the queue. Upon getting to my seat, I noticed a man sitting in the aisle seat, while mine was by the window. I guessed he was Irish, though I wasn't entirely sure. We exchanged greetings, and I was relieved to see that the middle seat remained vacant—it gave me some space to rest my arm. I hoped it would stay unoccupied, as I was exhausted after the long journey. Besides, whenever I have an early flight to catch, I hardly sleep the night before, worrying about missing it.

That morning, I had a bit of a situation while getting to LAX. I called my American-Korean friend, Connor, to pick me up, but I lied to him, telling him my flight was at 11 a.m. when in fact, it was at 1 p.m. I asked him to pick me up at 7 a.m. The poor lad arrived early, and we had quite a good time driving from Granada Hills to LAX. It was also our reunion, as we hadn't met since 2024, and now it was 2025. However, there was an accident on the freeway, causing a two-hour delay in traffic. Connor grew worried about whether I'd make it on time, since it's always advised to be at the airport three hours before a flight. It was already past 9 a.m., and we had two more hours to reach the airport, meaning we'd arrive around 11 a.m. Then I told Connor my flight was actually at 1 p.m. He was furious and said, "Bro, if your flight is at 1 p.m., we could have left at 10 a.m. and avoided the morning traffic jam. People travel for work in the morning, so it's always like this." I listened quietly and prayed.

In the end, getting to the airport early was a wise decision. By the time we arrived, it was already 11 a.m. If we had left at 10 a.m., we would have faced the same traffic issues. After all, it's Los Angeles.

With the sleepless night and stressful commute adding to the long layover at the Canadian airport, I thought having an empty seat next to me would be a privilege. Just then, I saw a beautiful English girl with black hair, elegantly dressed in a black coat, smiling as she approached. I just knew she would take the middle seat.

Whenever I travel on a plane, I always dress well, usually in a suit and tie. I appreciate seeing others do the same—it's a bit disappointing when people travel in pyjamas, as if they're heading to bed. I find it disrespectful, to be honest. Imagine if the flight attendants or even the pilot wore pyjamas.

Throughout the flight, I tried to sleep. As I said, I'm quite a shy person and don't talk much unless I feel like it. I slept for most of the journey, pressing myself towards the window, keeping nearly ten inches of space between me and the girl. I don't like accidentally touching a woman, so

I'd rather be uncomfortable myself to ensure she feels at ease.

I overheard her talking to the Irish man, though I wasn't paying much attention. However, as the wind carried her words to me, I caught that she owned a business. I took a long nap and woke up feeling much better just as the food was being served. I believe she ordered pasta, while I opted for beef. As I unpacked my meal, I carefully arranged everything neatly on my tray—water, dessert, cutlery, and so on. I started with the cheese and toast before moving on to the main course.

I noticed the girl next to me taking pictures of her food. Then, she handed me her cheese and said, "Would you like some cheese? I won't eat it anyway." It was a kind gesture, so I accepted, and she smiled. She was a very polite young lady.

After finishing my meal, I packed everything neatly, as I always like to keep my space clean. She did the same. I decided to go back to sleep, but a mild headache started creeping in. I thought it would pass if I took another nap.

At some point, I needed to use the loo. Being in the window seat has its perks for the view, but when nature calls, it's a bit inconvenient. The person in the middle and the aisle seat both have to get up just so you can pass. It's even worse if they're asleep.

In the middle of the night, when everyone was fast asleep, I woke up with a severe headache. I saw a flight attendant handing out tablets and water to someone behind me, but before I could get her attention, she was gone. I waited for a while and then pressed the call button. When she arrived, she immediately brought me a glass of water, understanding that I probably needed it. I whispered to ask for a headache tablet, not wanting to wake the girl next to me. However, she woke up anyway and tried to figure out what I was saying. Since the flight attendant couldn't hear me clearly, the girl relayed my request. The attendant asked if I was travelling alone and whether I had any allergies. Once she confirmed it was safe to give me the tablet, she brought it over. I took it and rested until morning.

As dawn broke, I noticed the beautiful colours outside the window. I took a few pictures and saw that she was awake.

Now that my headache had eased, I decided to strike up a conversation. I greeted her, and we shook hands as we introduced ourselves. She told me her name was Olivia—a very common English name, to be honest.

I asked her what brought her to London, and she simply replied, “Home.” Ah, what a lovely place to call home, I thought. I told her I was visiting my sister and her family and also planned to meet my mentors and producers. When she asked about my work, I shared details about my latest film script, which I had just finished writing. I wanted my producers and a few actor friends to review it. I even pulled out my red file from my bag so she could see the script for herself.

After a few days in cold London, I messaged her: “I’ve been checking out your work—it’s very impressive. Before you leave for Canada, we must catch up.”

She replied: “Oh, thank you! Yes, if my schedule allows, for sure. It’s a bit busy, but if some time clears up, we could make something work.”

And she was genuinely in London to visit her home. I recalled that she said she would be in London for just two weeks before returning to Canada, as she had to finish her college and had just 300 more days before returning to London for good. Or did she say she would be back in June or July? Something like that.

I'm still hoping to meet her again. You rarely come across such an elegant, well-mannered woman—someone with old-money charm and priceless etiquette. If you do, trust me, you'd better not lose that friendship.

4.

Screened by Fate.

Adventure, Ambition, Attraction.

A chance encounter at a film festival leads to an unforgettable connection.

Who doesn't love film festivals? For any aspiring filmmaker or seasoned veteran, film festivals are one of the most significant platforms to gain recognition, showcase your work, and connect with others in the industry. I've always believed in the magic they offer.

Back in 2017, as I neared the completion of filming *Welcome Millions,* one of my feature films shot in Goa, I decided to take a well-deserved week-long break before diving into post-production. Little did I know that this break would open the door to an unforgettable experience at the Film Festival in Goa.

Living in Cuncolim, I knew I'd have to travel to Panaji for the festival. Instead of commuting daily, I figured it would be far more convenient to book a hotel in the city. My production company in the UK was kind enough to cover all my expenses, ensuring I could attend the event without any worries. I had borrowed a scooter from my sister-in-law, to get around. However, there was one problem—I didn't have a driving license. Despite this, I figured my reputation and good connections with the local police might provide me with a little leniency if things went south.

For the duration of the festival, I attended screenings, interviews, and seminars hosted by renowned filmmakers. The focus of the festival was primarily on international and world cinema, and it was a truly enriching experience. It was amazing to think that such an incredible event was hosted right here in Goa—a blessing for the people of the region.

One afternoon, I found myself scanning the list of films scheduled for screening, determined to grab a ticket. The rule was straightforward—only registered delegates could pick up tickets at the cinema hall's booking counter. This counter was conveniently located in a charming part of Panaji, near the Latin Quarters, an area that exuded the same charm as Lisbon. If you've never visited Lisbon but have been to Goa, you're already familiar with the essence of Portugal.

By sheer luck, I managed to snag a ticket for one of the films. Most screenings had been sold out, and I was thrilled to have one available. Just before I joined the queue to pick up my ticket, I was interviewed by Flexcia D'Souza, a journalist. The attention felt a little surreal, but it added to the excitement of the day.

As I stood in line, I noticed a red carpet laid out for the cast and crew. Among them, I spotted a few well-known Bollywood actors and a stunning English woman. I couldn't help but guess that this film was a British production featuring some of India's biggest stars. I hadn't read the film synopsis before picking up the ticket; I had simply grabbed whatever was available.

Inside the cinema hall, I took a seat in the second row, right behind the cast and crew. Before the screening began, the host introduced the actors, the director, and the producer, presenting them with mementoes and inviting them to speak. The Bollywood actor spoke first, followed by the producer. But my attention was focused on the beautiful English lady—was she part of the cast? As it turned out, she was the director of the film. Shy and reserved, she didn't speak much about the film itself, encouraging the audience to watch it rather than hear a lengthy introduction.

When the film began, I was completely absorbed. It was a stunning English film shot in one of my favourite cinematic landscapes—England.

After the screening, most attendees rushed to take pictures with the Bollywood stars, while the young, beautiful English director stood off to the side, seemingly alone. I knew this was my chance—I couldn't let it slip away. I walked up to her, greeted her by name, and asked, "What are you doing later today? Fancy a cup of coffee with me?"

I had no idea why I asked that, but I liked her. To my surprise, she smiled and agreed. We snapped a picture together, and I told her how much I had enjoyed the film. She mentioned her plans for the evening, "I'll be leaving the cinema hall with the cast and producer, but I'll see you outside, and we can plan something."

She had actually accepted my invitation!

The problem was, she would be escorted out with her entourage, while I had to exit through the general public's exit. With the crowds outside, packed with multiple screening rooms and food stalls, I knew it would be nearly impossible for us to find each other again without exchanging contact information.

I rushed through the exit, trying to avoid the crowd. As I turned toward one of the food stalls, I spotted her in the middle of the venue, speaking to two men. The moment she saw me, her face lit up, and she quickly excused herself from the conversation. "Excuse me, I have to leave," she said, and walked straight toward me with a smile. "Great, you found me," she added.

She looked effortlessly elegant in a black dress, perfectly suited for a gala event. A refined English lady with blonde hair and an impeccable English accent.

Before we could sit down for coffee, she explained that she needed to find the travel agency, which puzzled me at first. She clarified that Festival Host had a travel desk responsible for arranging travel and accommodation for invited filmmakers. As her film had been selected for a premiere, she was one of the VIP guests managed by this agency.

We set off on a small adventure, moving from office to office, searching for the agency. After knocking on three different doors, we finally found it. She went inside to handle her business while I waited outside. The festival was set up in a closed-off area, with three main halls and multiple screening rooms, only accessible to registered delegates.

A few minutes later, she returned with a smile. "Ah, now it's time for coffee, but I'll have tea," she said. We headed to the nearest food stall and ordered our drinks.

As we sat together, she shared more about her experience. "My flight to London was scheduled for tomorrow, but I wanted to stay a little longer," she said. "I asked the travel agency to extend my stay for another ten days. Unfortunately, they can't keep me in the five-star hotel I'm staying at, but that's not a problem—one of the actor's friends has offered to host me at her house. So, I'll be here for the week, and we can plan something exciting."

It was a surreal moment—like a dream date with a celebrity film director! Of course, I wasn't any less accomplished myself, but I chose not to bring up my own career just yet. I was simply enjoying the company of someone I had just met.

I asked if she was free for dinner that evening, but she explained that she was moving to her actor friend's house and had to attend a pre-planned gala dinner with producers and event organisers. The next day was the festival's closing ceremony, which she also planned to attend. We agreed to meet on the third day, exchanged email addresses, and connected on Social Media network.

That night, after the closing ceremony—which I couldn't attend as it was by invitation only—I spent my evening watching films and returned to my hotel. I sent her a message on Social Media: "It was great meeting you at the Festival, keep shining, dear."

Her reply was brief: "Likewise x."

I then asked, "Are you still in Goa?" and told her about my film, which had just wrapped up and was about to enter post-production.

On the third day, she replied to my message: "Yes, I'm here today and tomorrow. Congratulations! I look forward to seeing it x." Later that same day, I left another message, but she didn't reply. I waited for three days, and on the fourth day, she messaged me: "Hey, I'm staying with someone in Mandur x."

Later that evening, on the fourth day, she messaged again: "Is Mandur near you? I leave on Monday x."

I replied, "I can make it to Mandur, let's meet. Mandur is closer than Panaji. Maybe we could plan for dinner?"

She then shared her number and asked if we could chat on Messaging App. That's when we began to plan. She sent me her address and asked if I could come by 9 am. She also asked if I had a car, and I said, "I'll come by scooter-bike. Do you want me to come by car?" She said, "Bike is fine." What a sweet lady.

I knew the area of Mandur well, as that's where my sister got married. I'd been there before and vaguely remembered the location; it was a beautiful village. Back then, we weren't using Digital Internet Maps for navigation—only to check routes—as Such a Digital Maps in Goa wasn't very up-to-date in 2017, at least not for me, as I had an Smart phone at the time. Ah, not very advanced.

So, Monday was the sixth day, but I could only see her on the fifth day. I borrowed my sister-in-law's scooter, had a spare helmet for her, and left quite early at 5:30 am, considering the distance from Cuncolim to Mandur, which would take about an hour by scooter. I arrived in Mandur at about 7 am, quite early, and waited until around 8 am to message her. When I did, she was already ready. I found the place she was staying at, picked her up, and we rode towards South Goa.

This English lady was very nice and polite. She didn't judge my scooter; all she was looking forward to was some fun time. I drove cautiously and safely, as I needed to take really good care of her. We arrived at Sernabatim Beach, I parked the scooter, and she asked if I wanted to wear swim trunks as she had brought some, surprisingly. I thought I wouldn't get into the water, as I was more interested in walking, so we walked along the coastline. Before that, we stopped at a nearby shack for coffee and sandwiches. I noticed the shoreline was rising, but I just ignored it, and we continued walking. We sat at a shack where the water was almost hitting the deck.

She had a DSLR camera and took lots of pictures of me, while I took some of her. We walked far along the coast, and after about 20 minutes, we reached another beach, somewhere close to Trinity Beach. If you look at it on a Map, you'll see how beautiful the coastline is. We found a lovely shack, had lunch, a few beers, and talked a lot about ourselves. That's when she mentioned her boyfriend. I was deeply interested in her until she mentioned him, and the gentleman's code was activated: "If she has a boyfriend, respect their relationship even more and ensure you don't disrupt something precious."

I honestly respect a girl who speaks the truth and keeps it real rather than hiding behind lies. She was a lovely lady, and after lunch, we walked back to the scooter. On the way, we saw a little dog, which she liked and played with. Then we sat on sunbeds; she had a beer while I stuck to sparkling water with lime, as I had to ride the scooter. We enjoyed our conversations. It could have meant something if she were single, but since she wasn't, it was still a very pleasant day. I then realised I'd left my scooter keys on the scooter while storing the helmet in the boot. I wasn't panicked, as I was confident no one would steal it—after all, it wasn't the first time this had happened.

We walked back to the scooter. I mentioned I had left the key on it, and it had been almost 8 hours since we'd been at the beach. When I got to the scooter, the key was still there, intact.

The next day was her flight to Bombay, so I wanted to get her home early so she could rest. On the way, she decided to buy flowers for the lady she was staying with, her actor friend. We also bought a cake, as she thought I could stay with her to have coffee and tea at the place she was staying.

When we reached Mandur, she said she would first ask permission to let me enter the room. The lady denied it, as she wasn't a Goan lady and didn't understand the culture. Additionally, she had some strange beliefs that no man's energy should be in her dwelling in the evening. Well, the English girl handed me the flowers and said, "These are for you," and told me to take the cake home. Our plans to spend the evening together were not quite fulfilled, so we bid goodbye at the gate.

I reached home at around 9 pm, and the first thing I saw was my mum waiting for me. At that time, my mum was old and not doing very well. She was a beautiful lady with a great heart, and I miss her dearly. As I entered, I handed her the bouquet of flowers. She loved them, and I took a picture and sent it to the English girl. After a few minutes, she said that if I was free tomorrow, I should come and spend time with her before she went to the airport in the evening. I told her I could come by car and arrange a taxi. We could spend some time together and then I'd drop her off at the airport. She liked that idea.

I knew one thing: she really liked me, and we had bonded well. The next day, I called a taxi driver, arranged the car for the day, and picked her up. The lady she was staying with didn't expect her to have someone else dropping her off at the airport, but never mind—this time, it was my turn.

The taxi driver thought she was my girlfriend because of the way we were bonding. He handed me his phone with some funny clips, I think from a comedian, while we were driving towards Vasco. As we watched the clips together in the back seat, I noticed she came really close to me. I could tell the driver saw this in his rearview mirror and probably thought we were going to kiss. I was aware that I mustn't get too close, but I knew there was something between us.

We reached a nearby restaurant, and as we got out, the driver said, "You're lucky to have someone like her." I didn't explain anything to him. He waited in the car as we walked into the restaurant to have a few drinks to say goodbye. She had two beers and said, "My actor friend, the lady I was staying with, didn't let me go anywhere, and I was stuck for three days. I wanted to meet you, but we've had a lovely time yesterday and today. I wish I had more time, more days." I replied, "I'll see you in London, don't worry, we'll meet again."

We then went to the airport. At the airport, she cracked a few jokes about the lady she was staying with, and we laughed. We hugged, and I said, "Can I see your passport?" Honestly, I just wanted to see how a British passport looked. I'm a Portuguese citizen, and I was curious if they were similar. Silly me. I saw it was almost the same, with her beautiful picture in it. We bid goodbye. We remained very good friends since then.

The next day, I read in the news about a weather warning regarding a possible earthquake in the middle of the ocean. I'm not sure of the cause, but they warned about a rise in the sea level that morning.

In 2018, I lost my mum; she passed away just before my trip to Los Angeles.

Eventually, in 2018, after my film premiered in Los Angeles and qualified for the 91st Academy Awards in the General Category (though it didn't make it to any nominations), I finally flew to London in 2019. As promised, we met there. She planned something interesting, but then I got news about Pandemic. It wasn't alarming at first, but I decided to fly back to Goa. The day before my flight, we met, and she told me she had just moved into a new apartment in London. She had planned dinner and wine, and invited me to stay for the night. But as I had to leave the next evening, I said, "Maybe next time."

I was carrying a small diary in which I would collect autographs from friends and people I consider dear. I asked her to sign it, and she wrote:

"See you next time when there's sun xx."

And signed.

I was so intrigued by her name and personality that when I became an uncle in 2019, following the birth of my sister-in-law's baby girl, the daughter of my eldest brother, I decided to be her godfather and named her after her.

5.

The Bollywood Encounter: A Friendship That Almost Was.

Friendship, Fame, Red Flags.

A chance meeting with a Bollywood star led to an unexpected bond, tested by time, values, and red flags.

I have been fortunate to meet many celebrities, and often, they became my friends. One particular encounter stands out in my memory—a moment that would unknowingly lead to an unexpected friendship.

I was working on one of my films, recording Dialogues in the studio while part of our team worked on the music score. Among us was a very famous celebrity—well-known to Indian audiences and abroad, a Bollywood Actress, the star of the highest calibre.

We had been formally introduced months earlier at an event. A month later, I emailed her, inviting her to contribute vocals for our film project. She was warmly received at the airport. At that time, I had recently met an English girl at the Film Festival, and for three days, our paths didn't cross. Those days were filled with post-production work.

That evening, the Bollywood star, our studio team, and I headed to a beach shack for dinner and drinks. I offered them whatever they wished to drink, remaining completely sober myself. She walked straight toward the shore. The beach shack was only a few metres from the shoreline, allowing guests to take their drinks right to the water's edge.

I wasn't particularly captivated by her fame, as I had little exposure to Bollywood, but the team was awestruck. Their excitement was palpable, while I remained indifferent. It was then that the *Gentleman's Code* was activated:

"Don't overwhelm a celebrity with the pressure of their fame—just act naturally and make her feel like an ordinary person. She'll appreciate the company since she's already experienced immense admiration. At some point, everyone needs a normal day."

After dinner, we dropped her off at her hotel. I informed her that I'd see her the following day, as interviews with a few journalists had been scheduled.

Once the interviews concluded, my thoughts shifted back to the English girl from the Film Festival. I had been eager to see her again, but she hadn't responded to my messages. Meanwhile, the celebration with the Bollywood star had gone exceptionally well, and soon, it was time to take her to the airport.

I felt no pressing need to stay in touch with her. I wasn't particularly drawn to her, nor was I aware of the magnitude of her fame, unlike everyone else around me, who were left in awe. Perhaps she wasn't used to being treated like an ordinary person by someone in the film industry.

A month later, I received an unexpected message from her on Social media:
"I'm coming to Goa tomorrow. Are you around?"
I responded, *"Yes, I am very much in Goa."*
She replied, *"Okay, I'll send you my flight details. Let's meet."*

And just like that, the unforeseen friendship began. I picked her up from the airport, and during her two-day stay, we explored both well-known and hidden corners of Goa.

Whenever she had a Bollywood project requiring travel, she ensured Goa was a stopover. She would insist her manager plan her flights so she could spend three days in Goa before heading to Bombay.

Over time, our friendship deepened. I had always sought good company—someone like her. Deep down, I knew I was developing feelings, but I didn't want to acknowledge them.

My faith was important to me; I had always imagined dating a Christian. This wasn't supposed to be a romantic relationship, yet it somehow became one. She often wondered why I never expressed my emotions.

A year later, one evening, a random Goan stranger messaged me. He was a die-hard fan of the Bollywood star and wanted to meet her. I had seen him before at some Social events, but we had never interacted. In Goa, however, no one is truly a stranger. If someone wishes to meet someone, we usually make it happen.

I mentioned the request to the Bollywood star, and she agreed. We arranged a dinner at *Goodfellas Italian Restaurant* in Benaulim. Fancy name, isn't it? They also served amazing pizzas.

The three of us met at the restaurant. She and I both had scooters, while the stranger arrived by car. Her hotel was within walking distance.

We enjoyed fancy cocktails and ordered pizza. Almost immediately, we became friends with the Goan stranger.

Throughout the evening, she seemed troubled by something—perhaps the emotions she was struggling with.

At one point, I excused myself to visit the toilet, leaving the two of them alone. I took about five to seven minutes, briefly chatting with a waitress. Upon my return, I sensed a shift in the atmosphere. Something serious had happened. Both the Bollywood star and the stranger looked tense, their conversation heavy with unspoken words.

What had just unfolded in my absence?

We all kept quiet, looking at each other's faces and ignoring the topic. Suddenly, she said she would be back in a minute, leaving us gentlemen at the table. The man then asked, "Is everything okay?" and I replied, "I was supposed to ask the same." He continued, "She's totally into you, and maybe you don't notice that." Just then, she returned, smiling and sounding happy, and said, "Hey Milroy, there's a girl by the WC, her name is Summer, and she is very much into you. She says she likes you. Why don't you go near the washing basin? There's a mirror there; she's there." For a moment, I was a little tense, wondering what this was about. Just to please her and go along with her game, I went to check.

There was nobody. All I could see were the waitresses moving around, so I decided to wash my hands at the wash basin. Looking at myself in the mirror, I saw the Bollywood Girl. She came up behind me and said, "Hello, I'm Summer." I responded, "Yes, I can see you are much hotter than Summer." We laughed. I didn't make it obvious that I understood the game but acted dumb as if I wasn't getting what it was about. I knew she meant to say she loved me. But the usual Gentleman's Code gets activated: "If you are not ready for the commitment, and she proposes indirectly, pretend you didn't quite catch the feather in the air." We men never like to be direct about it.

That evening was very awkward. I was so worried about stepping into a relationship and commitment, as I was purely intent on dating a Christian girl. My objectives were clear, but this Bollywood Girl was a chance encounter. I never intended to exploit this friendship by turning it into a relationship. Gentleman's Code: "If you're not ready for a relationship or commitment, don't exploit her feelings. Instead, exercise restraint and maintain some distance to reflect. Feelings are precious, as is respect."

Just as a timeless, priceless wristwatch not only tells time but also reminds you of your standards, status, and accomplishments, it is equally important to maintain such standards when dealing with people. I believe in keeping a clean image. Another reason could be my Pai (Dad). He was a very well-respected man in town—so much so that even when I had no money to buy a book during my school days, I could go to the stationery shop and tell the owner that my dad would pay in the evening, and they would immediately trust me and hand it over. He was a strict man, neat, very much a businessman, and a true gentleman.

That evening, as we left the Italian restaurant, she drove her scooter, and so did I, while the stranger man left in his car. The Bollywood Girl and I ended up at her hotel room. I thought it was necessary to tell her what I really felt about her and our friendship. We sat opposite each other in the room, and I said, "Listen, I respect that you have feelings for me, and as much as you do, so do I. But there is something you need to know about me, as you know nothing." She interrupted, "We've known each other for a year. I know you well." I replied, "You know what I have let you know, but hear me out." I continued, "I am Christian, and my faith in Jesus is my foundation. I don't want you to feel the religious gap, but that is how I see things. I would date and marry a Christian. I am not interested in making up a relationship for fun. I know very well where this is heading, knowing your religious views. I respect yours, and I believe you have put a lot of trust in me. I appreciate that."

I made her understand all my reasons for pausing. I'm sure she understood, and as dawn approached, I had a sleepless night. I thought I should head back home. I left, and we decided to meet later that evening.

The stranger Goan man was no longer a stranger and became a good friend. He came to visit her that afternoon as he was curious about what was going on between us. We had coffee together, and such incidents continued—meeting all three of us at different places.

One evening, he wanted to drop me off home. While we were driving, I recall him saying, "She loves you very much, and I think you don't really see it." I told him briefly what he should know to avoid digging deeper into the topic, and we parted ways.

The Bollywood Girl and I didn't end our friendship; instead, it continued growing even stronger. Our bond of friendship eventually made me a bit more popular within the elite circles of Bollywood actors and singers because she often talked about me and my work and acknowledged that she had a friend in Goa. Goa is considered one of the most prominent destinations that everyone truly adores, especially the elites in Bollywood.

We continued meeting each other, and over time, I began to notice many things—some of which I'd like to highlight. She was super polite, nice, and very humble towards me. Often, we visited fancy restaurants and beachside shacks. There were incidents that made me reflect deeply on where I was stepping into.

Once, we went to a Greek restaurant and ordered a very popular Greek dessert and wine. When the dessert was served, after one bite, she called the attention of the waitress. When the waitress came, she asked, "Did you prepare this dish here?" The waitress replied, "Yes, we have a pastry chef." She then insisted on calling the chef.

The chef came, and I must say, everyone there almost knew me, as I was already popular, and so was she. The staff were Goan. She insulted the chef, telling him that she had been to Greece last month, had the same dish, and it didn't taste exactly as it should. The chef explained that some ingredients found in Greece taste different from those found here. It turned into an argument, as she wanted to prove her point. I felt very embarrassed, knowing that we were not here to be Gordon Ramsay. A red flag slowly appeared. You might wonder why this should be considered a red flag. Well, you'll see. The restaurant didn't charge us for that dessert. That's what I noticed on the bill —it wasn't charged.

As our friendship grew even further, once we were at a shack having dinner, and she called her mum on a video call. She said, "Mum, I'm with Milroy, having dinner." I felt nice that her mum knew about me. Her mum greeted me over the video call that evening. It was a sweet gesture. She always felt safe with me, even when we drove around late at night.

One evening, I remember we were at a famous shack in Colva, right by the shore, facing the sea. The sound of the gusting waves was so relaxing, and we had ordered fancy mocktails. As the waiter brought them to us, we began to sip and enjoy the ambience. Some time later, she noticed a tiny insect in her drink. Given that we were in a tropical climate, by the seashore at dusk, with the wind blowing and insects around, this was quite expected.

However, instead of addressing the issue politely, she instantly caught the waiter's attention and reacted with anger and aggression, complaining as if the presence of the tiny insect had been deliberate. She insisted he bring her a new drink. I felt terrible. As the waiter walked towards the bar with her drink, I seized the moment, walked up to him, tapped him on the shoulder, and apologised on her behalf.

He looked deeply upset and said, "She argued as if the little insect was deliberately put in. Considering you're sitting outside, it's obvious these things can happen."

I nodded in understanding. In my mind, I thought she could have simply picked the tiny insect out and continued drinking or, at the very least, requested a replacement politely—she would have received it anyway.

Gentleman's Code: "You can tell a lot about a person by how they treat the waiter."

One of the things I do when I have a business meeting is to host it over coffee, lunch, or dinner. This allows me to observe how a person sits, how they eat, how they treat others at the table, and, most importantly, how they treat the waiter. Small things, but they make quite an impact when analysing how they would eventually treat you.

With this Bollywood girl, I knew for sure how she would eventually treat me. That was when the red flag became prominently visible. Although I had a great deal of respect for her, I began to count the red flags—a way to send a message to my heart to stay alert.

Our friendship lasted for five years as we gradually drifted apart. Eventually, I moved to Los Angeles, California, to begin my journey in Hollywood.

What I can say about this experience is that not every friendship should turn into a relationship. For various reasons, it is good to understand a person for a very long time. The quickest way to pick up red flags is through situations at cafés or restaurants. Etiquette matters—at least to me—and it reflects the true nature of a person.

6.

The Meeting That Changed Everything.

Friendship Beyond Borders.

A journey of unexpected connections, deep conversations, and enduring friendships.

I was first introduced to the famous app to meet Travellers while working on the post-production of my film *Welcome Millions* in 2017. Subivk, a young gentleman from Kerala, was kind enough to say that I'd connect with amazing people on app, given my personality.

My first encounter was during the summer in Goa. One morning, I received a message on that app from a man named Edwin, hailing from some parts of South America. His purpose for using the app was to connect with tourists visiting Goa and learn about their cultures. Goa is a popular tourist destination, known for its rich European influences and unique, diverse cultures. Some even call it the "Europe of India"—and rightly so.

I had messaged several tourists who were listed as either visiting or already in Goa with a simple note: "Hey, welcome to Goa. Just a small gesture, I'd like to invite you to our Chat group, where I host a few surfers for an evening of beers." I sent them the link to the group.

Edwin replied, and I learned that he was traveling with a friend, Sonya. I instantly assumed she must be Goan, as her last name was a common surname in my neighbourhood, and Sonya is a typical Goan name. Goa has deep Portuguese influence, so Spanish or Latin surnames were not unusual.

Nrupen, my manager, and I drove to the bus stop near my village to pick up Edwin and Sonya. I greeted Sonya in Konkani, but she didn't quite understand. She then spoke to Edwin in Spanish, a language I understood well given my Portuguese roots. I responded, 'Sonya, ¿Hablas Español?' When I asked where she was from, she said she was from California—a Californian girl who looked like she had Goan roots, undoubtedly due to her Spanish-Mexican ancestry. They made a lovely couple, and it was a pleasure to meet them. All the possible gentlemen's codes were activated, with the code being: "Don't steal someone else's love interest, even if it hasn't yet flourished."

They had booked a reservation in Canacona, near Palolem Beach, a lovely area with a small Jewish community and synagogue. I took them to a nearby restaurant for a lovely lunch with drinks, which they were quite happy to have.

While waiting for our food, Sonya showed me a wound on her arm and asked, "Milroy, do you know what this is?" I recognised it immediately. It was a mark left by a Nexplanon contraceptive implant. My best friend Ashley had told me about it before. It's a small, thin rod, about the size of a matchstick, that is inserted under the skin, and when removed, it leaves a scar. Sonya's implant had only been removed a few days ago, and it was still sore and bleeding. Nrupen was surprised as he'd never heard of it, but I explained. Sonya shared a similar experience in Jaipur, where her hosts were equally fascinated by the implant.

After lunch, we dropped them off at their guesthouse and made plans to hang out the next day.

The following day, Edwin and Sonya made their way directly to my place, following Digital Navigational Maps. Nrupen wasn't available, so I called Amit, a well-known rapper in Goa who went by the name "Waking Grunt." Amit was a good friend, and I thought he'd be great company. It took him nearly 40 minutes to arrive, and by then, Edwin decided to take the wheel and drive us around. Since driving in Goa is on the left side, Edwin found it confusing, especially when he accidentally turned on the windshield wipers instead of the indicator, nearly swerving into the next lane. I decided it was best to return home and wait for Amit.

When Amit finally arrived, we drove to Betul by the riverside, enjoyed some drinks, and relaxed. Later, I took them to a party at "Southerndeck," a popular shack in Colva with a DJ and good food. The evening was eventful, and I unexpectedly met a Internet friend, Zubin, a journalist, who joined us for dinner. I got into a discussion about LGBTQ issues with Sonya, which got her a bit upset, as my Christian values didn't align with some of the topics. We eventually changed the subject to Goan food, and after dinner, we hit the dance floor. Zubin left, and we had a blast dancing to the DJ's beats.

After the drinks and food, we were all somewhat tipsy. Amit, who hadn't been drinking, drove them back to their guesthouse, and I ended up vomiting as soon as I stepped out of the car to bid goodbye to them. That was the last time I drank, and I vowed never to drink again.

The next day, with a slight hangover, I knew it would be their last day in Goa. They messaged me their live location, and we made plans to meet in Margão. I tracked their bus, although the live location wasn't updating correctly, and relied on my instincts.

Once in Margão, we met up with Nrupen and had a delicious Goan lunch—fish curry, fried fish, and rice. Sonya teased me about the previous night's incident, and we all laughed. Sonya and Edwin were somewhat dating, but I could tell Edwin was more serious about it. Sonya, on the other hand, saw their relationship as more of a travel partnership. She was a kind and knowledgeable traveler, and I noticed she wore a Hebrew alphabet necklace. When I asked what it meant, she explained it was a gift from a woman, and the letter symbolised life.

Edwin, in contrast, was looking for deeper love. He was humble, protective, and had a strong, steady presence. After lunch, they left for their next destination, an island in the Philippines.

After the Goa carnival, the pandemic hit. Edwin called me one day to tell me that Sonya had been sent back to the

United States after being reported as a foreigner in the Philippines. Edwin managed to stay in the country, but Sonya was deported. I could feel the emotional distance between them growing, and it was heartbreaking to witness their unspoken separation.

Despite the distance, they both stayed in touch with me but wanted to keep their friendship separate. Edwin eventually found love during the lockdown with a Canadian woman. Sonya, meanwhile, was in California, bonding with her family. It was nice to see her happy and surrounded by loved ones.

Eventually, the pandemic restrictions were lifted, and Edwin was able to return to South America, while the Canadian girl went back to Canada. I was planning to visit the United States, but my brother and I opened a café during the lockdown, and travel plans were put on hold.

One morning, I received a devastating message from Edwin. A fire had broken out in Canada, where his girlfriend was living, and while her family was saved by firefighters, she tragically perished in the disaster. Edwin was heartbroken, and I genuinely believed he had found true love in her.

A year later, I was in California and reached out to Sonya. We spent the day together, playing golf, visiting the Getty Museum, and having lunch. Sonya reminded me of the time I had thrown up at the party, and I told her that I had been sober for two years.

Sonya and I remain friends till this day, and though Edwin and I rarely stay in touch, we occasionally check each other's social media to keep tabs on one another.

This experience was one of the most extraordinary of my life, and I consider Sonya a true friend. While I haven't met Edwin in person since, Sonya and I have plans to meet again, as she still lives in California.

7.

The Night I Doubted Trust.

Trust. Doubt. Escape.

A filmmaker, a stranger, and a dangerous game.

Film directors have the power to make anyone popular—that is one of the beliefs aspiring actors hold. And in a way, it is true; we create. I recall one such unexpected encounter. At the time, I was quite popular—constant media attention, Page 3 parties, events, awards—you name it. I was also in the process of writing a film script, having just been signed by a film production company based in England. It was their debut film, and I was set to direct it, somewhere around the year 2014. I had just been verified on Social Media—back when verification "blue tick badge" wasn't a paid feature but was granted purely on merit.

At that time, I had a girlfriend. It was a fragile relationship, something I probably shouldn't have stepped into.

I frequently received messages from Social Media followers, many of whom sought guidance on breaking into the film industry. Among them was a girl from Calcutta named Priya. She was deeply fascinated by films and stardom; she wanted to be a star. She would occasionally call me, asking for advice on how to start a career in films. It wasn't unusual—I had many people contacting me for similar reasons.

One evening, I received a call from Priya. She informed me that she was on a train to Goa—an entirely unplanned trip —and wanted me to pick her up from the station that night. I mentioned this to my girlfriend at the time, explaining that since this girl was arriving in Goa for the first time, the least I could do was arrange for my driver to pick her up and drop her at her hotel. I thought I would host her for dinner as a courtesy. Little did I know how troublesome this would become.

I waited outside the train station with my driver, our car parked near the entrance. Eventually, I saw a young girl, probably around nineteen, with a small bag slung over her shoulder. Behind her were four young men, following closely. They looked like they were from a rural part of India—lacking manners and self-respect, evident in their walk and gestures. As she approached, she waved them goodbye. I asked, "Are they with you?" She replied that they were fellow passengers she had just met on the train. That was understandable, but when she asked if they could join us in the car, I firmly refused. "They aren't really your friends, right? You just met them," I pointed out. "Let me drop you at your hotel. But first, we can have dinner."

Gentlemen Code: "If a woman speaks or behaves inelegantly, guide her towards a path of ethics that align with your manners. Do not descend into the dirt with her."

As we drove towards the beach, it was already late—around 9 p.m. She expressed a desire to visit a beachside shack, having never seen one before. On the way, I asked where her hotel was so I could plan something nearby, as I needed to be home by 10 p.m. The next morning, my producers in England were scheduled to call for a script update, and I had a packed schedule.

To my shock, she admitted she hadn't booked a hotel and had no money to book one. That was a problem. She was a young woman alone in a new city, and I couldn't just abandon her in the middle of the night. I assured her that I would figure something out, and she immediately looked relieved.

She then asked me to stop by a gypsy store—one of the many small roadside shops common along Colva Beach Road. She insisted I buy her a dress. I knew those stores were inexpensive, so I agreed, purchasing one for around INR 500 (about USD 5). Meanwhile, I asked my driver if he knew of a budget-friendly hotel where she could stay for the night. She had planned to leave the next day by train back to Calcutta.

I never wanted to be in such a tricky situation. On one hand, my relationship was already strained. My girlfriend had high expectations of me—assuming that, as a filmmaker, I had a lot of money. The reality was that I was banking on this big film project. Completing the script and moving into production was crucial for my career. I had no time for distractions like this. However, I was also aware of my public image. Leaving Priya stranded could lead to legal or media complications, especially if someone had spotted us together. I had to be extremely cautious.

My driver suggested a discreet hotel where I wouldn't likely be recognised. But as I approached the reception, the gentleman at the counter immediately recognised me. And there it was—the beginning of an ordeal I had not anticipated.

I booked a room for her, helped her settle in, and ensured it was clean. Then, I waited outside while she freshened up and changed into the dress I had bought her.

Later, we walked down to the beach and found a shack. The setting was beautiful—a candlelit table, the scent of the ocean in the air, tables and chairs set on the sand at a distance from the shore. The sound of waves, the cool breeze, and the moonlight created an enchanting atmosphere. It wasn't a date, but that's just how beach shacks in Goa are—romantic by default.

I had no idea how the night would unfold, but I was certain this was not going to be a simple encounter.

As we ordered our food, I noticed she was busy texting back and forth, either on Social Media Messenger or other messaging apps. She wanted to have a beer, so I asked her age. She claimed she was 19, but she looked more like 18—I was sure she was lying. I said, "No, no beer for a girl your age, and not with me." She scoffed, "Why are you acting like a dad?" Well, at least she had some idea of the pressure I was under.

As we were having dinner, I heard voices behind me. I turned around and saw the same young men I had spotted at the train station. Now, this isn't about being prejudiced, but in Goa, we don't particularly appreciate ill-mannered Indian tourists. I was surprised to see them there and suspected she had messaged them. Then she asked, "Can they join us for dinner?"

I was taken aback. She added, "They don't have money. Can you help?" I refused outright. We finished our dinner, and I noticed that the men were sitting far away from the shack, under the moonlight, in the darkest area where the waves gently lapped at the shore. Some drunk men nearby had completely lost their senses. It was not a safe place for a girl like her.

Priya said her friends were calling her to join them. She urged me, "At least once, try to blend in with normal people. I know you're a famous person, but it's fun to be among the ordinary." I had good connections with the police, and I sensed trouble. To be prepared for any unforeseen event, I texted an officer, sharing my location and brief details about where and whom I was with. I alerted him in case of an emergency. The officer had already informed his colleagues, who were patrolling the vicinity—at least, that's what I assumed.

As we approached the group, I noticed they were shabbily dressed, while she and I were quite well-dressed. They glanced at me and instantly judged me as a posh guy. They had a bottle of alcohol with them and were sitting on the ground. Some of them ran into the water, and she instantly joined them, playing in the waves. They made her drink straight from the bottle. I noticed this immediately and called out to one of them, telling him to stop. He walked up to me, offering me a sip. I refused. He laughed and said, "You're a Goan, and you don't fancy alcohol?"

It's quite common for Indians to assume that Goans drink alcohol all the time, since it's tax-free in Goa. Most Indian tourists tend to drink to empty as many alcohol bottles as they can buy cheaply. However, among Goans, beer, wine, and other alcoholic beverages are typically present during special occasions. It's normal for Goans to have wine at dinner, but many outsiders exaggerate this assumption and believe that Goans are constantly drinking.

I refused again, and then I saw the others misbehaving with her. I couldn't tolerate it. By this time, she had already downed half the bottle. While I was confronting the guy, she slurred, "They're my friends." The situation went on for about twenty minutes. I tried to keep her by my side to prevent the drunken boys from misbehaving. She was completely sloshed—she could barely stand. I told them firmly, "Hey, the party's over. It's time to go home."

I took her and walked straight to the hotel, which was just a minute away. The beach was part of the hotel premises. One of the men looked at me as if I were taking her to bed. They weren't happy that I had taken her away.

All I wanted was to end the night. As soon as we reached the room, she felt nauseous, rushed to the toilet, and vomited. She completely lost her balance and could barely move—she was heavily intoxicated. I had to put her to bed. Just as I was about to leave, there was a knock on the door. I opened it, ready to step out, when suddenly, these men stormed into the room.

They surrounded the bed. There were four of them. They ignored me entirely and started talking to her. She, still intoxicated, mumbled, "Let's party." I couldn't tolerate this —I was afraid things could turn ugly.

A table stood beside her bed, holding a water bottle and two empty glasses. As I reached for my mobile, I dialled the officer's number. He answered, but I said nothing. Instead, I looked straight at the men and warned them, "Hey, you better leave this room now."

One of them glanced at the empty glass, and I felt he was about to grab it—this could end badly. I raised my phone and said, "I don't know what she told you, but for sure, you don't know who I am. I've called the police. If you don't leave this room in the next minute, be prepared to face the consequences."

I was a big fan of Jack Reacher and all the Tom Cruise movies. Oh, let me tell you something fascinating—Tom Cruise has been following me on my social media since the time my film premiered in Los Angeles. That fan moment has stuck with me, influenced by all his movies.This situation felt straight out of one of those films—I was playing with their minds. In reality, I had no control over the situation: four men, one intoxicated girl, and a hotel room. And the gentleman's code was activated: "If you find yourself in a situation beyond your control, turn their own minds against them."

In no time, they stormed out of the room, fear evident in their eyes. I shut the door firmly behind them.

From the bed, she slurred, "Why did you do that? They're my friends."

I wasn't sure at that moment whether they had genuinely known her or if they had just coincidentally met on the train. All I cared about was her safety—the room was booked under my name.

I was deeply worried. If I left, would she be safe? What if she vomited in her sleep? I recalled the haunting scene from *Breaking Bad* Season 2, where Jesse's girlfriend, Jane, flipped onto her back, asphyxiated on her own vomit, and died from an overdose.

I sat there, contemplating my next move, as the waves outside crashed gently against the shore.

I got a call from the police officer, and I explained the situation to him. He said that since the room was booked under my name, if anything went awry, it would be a very worrisome situation. He advised me to leave, but I wasn't ready to go until she was back to her senses and feeling alright. I gave her some lemon juice and noticed that her phone kept ringing.

Several hours later, I sat on a chair near the door, watching her sleep. I was texting my girlfriend, explaining the situation, and then I called her up and spoke to her at midnight. Returning to the chair, I sat quietly. As soon as she began to feel better, she stood up on her own. I moved to help her, but she said, "Don't."

She went to the toilet, and I told her not to latch the door, just in case she fell. But she locked it anyway. After a while, she came out looking fresh—she had taken a shower. It was about time for me to leave. Dawn had just broken when she saw her phone, filled with several missed calls and text messages. She looked at me and asked, "What happened last night? Why are my friends terrified?"

At around 7 a.m., we sat at the restaurant café by the beach. I called my driver to pick me up while we had breakfast. I noticed those boys lingering a little away from the hotel café. She messaged them her location once again and then turned to me.

"Why are my friends terrified? What did you do to them?"

After breakfast, I suggested, "Let's take a walk on the beach while my driver arrives."

As we walked, I said, "If I tell you what happened last night, you wouldn't believe me. So, for your own good, return to the train station, board that train, and go home." I continued, "If you want to pursue a film career, don't ever make this mistake again. Study well, complete your education, learn about films, and you'll find an opportunity someday."

She looked at me and asked, "Would you cast me in your films?"

I smiled and replied, "Definitely... not."

Those boys lingered in the distance like shadows. As I was walking away, bidding her goodbye, she went to them and spoke in hushed tones. When I reached my car, I thought I'd call her before leaving. She approached the window, and I rolled it down.

"Do you want me to drop you off at the train station?" I asked.

She shook her head. "I'll go with my friends."

I didn't say anything. Instead, I asked if she had enough money for the train ticket. She hesitated, and I could tell she didn't. So, I handed her enough to cover the fare, then drove off.

Looking back now, it seems to me that they were all in on it together. But she trusted those boys more than me, so it was pointless to explain the entire situation. I was exhausted from staying up all night and just wanted to leave.

I never contacted her again, and from that day, I never stopped doubting the people I met. There's one thing about Goans—we trust people easily. Goa, being a tourist hub, is always filled with new faces, and we welcome them with open arms.

That morning, I returned home straight into a meeting with the producer over the phone. My focus had already shifted back to my film preparations.

Eventually, the film marked great success. As I mentioned, Tom Cruise followed me on one of my social media handles, which was something I treasured. Then, the popular Danish band, *Michael Learns to Rock*—which is extremely famous in Goa and other parts of Asia, and a band I grew up listening to—contributed to the film's original soundtrack.

By God's grace, despite all the changes in direction, I was put on a better track instead of getting derailed. The success of the film sparked media attention, and I became quite well known.

Tragically, much before my film could be completed in post-production, my girlfriend broke up with me, as she found a better future for herself—and I appreciate that.

Gentlemen's Code

The origins of the codes were formed at the dinner table with my church friend on the night we were celebrating our small group's Christmas dinner at a wonderful restaurant called *Majordomo* in Los Angeles, California. James, one of our church members and part of our group, was there. These small groups are organised based on age, and anyone between 25 and 40 would belong to ours.

James and I bonded well as we had something in common. Anthony, a childhood friend of James, brought up various vivid situations, and we all shared our stories. While sharing my experiences, I often used the catchphrase *"Gentleman's Code."*

I'm sure that if they read this book—well, eventually they will—they'll find the stories in much more detail. At the dinner table, they weren't as detailed as they are here, and they didn't hear all of them.

I only shared three out of the seven stories, and even those weren't brief.

I remember saying, *"Well, my life has been interesting, and most of the stories I'm about to share are like short films."*

Quotes and the meaning:

1. ***That was clearly just a lipstick stain on a coffee mug.*** "It refers to the lipstick stain left on mugs in a restaurant or café, making it difficult to determine whose it was—merely leading to assumptions about who might have left it."

2. ***..there were many men around the area, usually taxi drivers or bike pilots.*** Did you know that in Goa, the two-wheel taxi drivers—on bikes—are called "Pilots"?

About the Author

Milroy Goes is a Portuguese-Goan, Los Angeles-based filmmaker, widely recognised for his contributions to cinema and the entertainment industry. After establishing his company, he has played a pivotal role in film production and distribution. He also had a stroke of luck at *The Academy Awards®*, qualifying his film for consideration, which helped establish him as a filmmaker with a global perspective. Since then, he has become a voting member of the *EMMY® Awards* and an active member of the *Television Academy®*.

Milroy is deeply involved in the arts—sketching, painting, writing film scripts, directing films, music videos, commercial advertisements, and cultural projects—bringing creative storytelling to life across multiple mediums. His work reflects a unique blend of artistic vision and business acumen, establishing him as a notable figure in the industry.

This book marks his debut as an author, adding to his extensive experience in writing film scripts.

9 788194 828501

Printed at Repro India Ltd.